Grace Takes Me

David J. Thompson

ISBN: 978-0-9992103-4-5

For Dave and Marion

"Ruin sometimes adds beauty . . ."
-Walker Evans

"I had nothing to offer anyone except my own confusion."
-Jack Kerouac

Content:

How Much She Was Showing

You gotta be fucking kidding me, Cyndy,
was all I heard, then something heavy slam
against the wall. I didn't dare turn away
from the tv as he clomped down the stairs,
and slammed the front door. I watched
his truck pull out of the driveway, knew
it had to be my housemate's new boyfriend,
Tim or Tom, some young guy who played
shortstop on her rec league softball team.

She came downstairs slowly a few hours later
with a pillow, a blanket, and a box of Kleenex.
Mind if I watch the game with you? she asked,
her voice a little thick, if I could use a little company.
Sure, I replied. There's beer in the fridge. She told me
no, said she was going to give up drinking for a while,
spread herself out on the couch. Whatever, Cyn, I said.
Knock yourself out, and then she started to cry.

Some Unitarian guy did the ceremony for free
out in the backyard under the trees a few months later.
A bunch of us grad students kicked in for a cake
from Kroger and some bottles of cheap champagne.
We switched to beer after the bride and groom left,
chatted around the picnic table as evening came on.
Somebody said with a sigh that everything had gone
pretty well even if Cyndy was really starting to show,
and the rest of us just sat there noiselessly nodding in the dark.

WESTERN FLYER

Grace Takes Me

In heaven, there's no such thing as time.
It's always a slow Saturday morning
with hazelnut coffee on the couch
while Grace Kelly makes French toast
in the kitchen. She serves it with a dusting
of confectioner's sugar and thick maple syrup
wearing only that lovely nightgown she shows
Jimmy Stewart in *Rear Window*. When I finish
eating, Grace takes me by the hand and softly
leads me back to the bedroom with none
of that crappy harp music playing in the background,
just Chet Baker blowing cool as can be.

Jimmy D's
BAR & GRILL
★ALL LADY'S★
DRINK'S FOR $5
★LIVE DJ★

Twenty, Thirty, Forty . . .

Twenty's great and thirty's even better,
he tells me in between puffs on his cigarette.
By forty, he continues as I rearrange my napkin,
things are still kind of okay, but fifty's bad, real bad.
He takes a swig from his longneck Budweiser;
I stare at my plate, a piece of hamburger bun
and scattered French fries smeared with ketchup.
And sixty? He asks almost like it's a question
he expects me to answer. Shit. I can't do anything
anymore. He puts out his cigarette, takes another
from a pack of Camel filters. Before he can light it,
I stand and pull on my coat. He asks if I'm leaving,
says the night's still young. I look at my watch, tell him
that it's already pretty damn late, much later than I thought.

El Rancho
Verde
MOTEL

Penelope

He's in line at Rite-Aid just to pick up
his prescription, the cashier's this old squat
woman with a low forehead and hair
like a chunk of worn steel wool
who moves like she's ten months pregnant.
When he sees that the name tag on her
blue smock says Penelope he wants
to ask her how Telemachus is doing,
if she's heard from Odysseus lately,
and if the pain-in-the-ass suitors are
still falling for that old unraveling
the weaving gag, but instead he just
pays the bill and smiles weakly at her
because he knows he doesn't have time to chat.
He has a stack of essays to grade
before tomorrow's classes, has to drive
through traffic to the grocery store
and the cleaners, drop off some
overdue videos before he gets
home to some leftover pizza
and Lite beer in his apartment.

Really Good Friends

She jumped on my lap,
my friend says, as soon
as her husband left for
another bottle of vodka.
She started kissing me.
I unbuttoned her blouse.
We were going at it pretty
good when he walked back
in because he forgot his wallet
or something. There I was
with her boobs in my face
and him standing there
with his hands in his pockets.
I asked him to forgive us, tried
to blame it on all the damn
drinking we were doing
in those days. He shook
his head, asked me to leave
before things could get any worse.

My friend sighed, got quiet
for a few seconds. I thought
his story was over. Then he
said, real loud, But we were
friends, *really good friends,*
in a voice between a prayer
and a question he knew
could never be answered.

ASHLEY
PENTECOSTAL
- CHURCH -
¼ MILE
HAVE BUILDING - NEED SAINTS
HAVE JESUS - NEED SINNERS
HAVE LOVE - NEED LONELY
HAVE HOPE - NEED HOPELESS

I Once Saw God Fishing

I once saw God fishing off a little bridge
over the Wabash near New Harmony, Indiana.
He looked a lot like my Uncle Harry
who worked for the phone company
in Baltimore for forty years before he retired
to a beachfront condo in Ocean City, Maryland.
I thought about stopping just to say hi,
see if he was catching anything, ask what he was using
for bait, but I was in a big hurry
to get to a friend's wedding in Kentucky,
so I decided I just didn't have the time.
I regret that now because Uncle Harry died
last November, and I haven't seen God,
fishing or otherwise, in a long, long time.

JESUS R. VEGA

Like The Nothing Of West Texas

On the highway between Pecos and Fort Stockton
while he was thinking he'd never seen nothing
quite like the nothing of West Texas,
she turned down the tape deck
and asked, *Did you think that
last winter was an easy time for me?*

The first time she'd asked he'd been stuck for an answer,
only knowing that watching her two-step
with the local cowboys at the motel lounge
back in Carlsbad the night before
hadn't exactly been easy for him.

So this time he replied *No, I guess not,*
Not feeling anything, thinking, *Jesus,
this really is the middle of nowhere.*

TROUBLED?
TRY PRAYER
T?TP

Lazarus

You've probably heard of me.
My name is Lazarus. I felt like hell
for years – achy all the time, nasty cough,
couldn't keep food down, trouble breathing.
Add to that my two nutty sisters, Martha
and Mary, who just drive me absolutely crazy.
It's no wonder neither of them can find a husband
and get out of my hair, they're too busy following
this new Jesus The Savior guy around. They brought him
by one weekend and he was okay, kind of quiet,
didn't eat or drink too much, but I didn't see
what the big deal was. I was really hoping
he was going to take one of them off my hands,
but he just told me he was sorry I was feeling
so bad and to hang in there, and then he was gone
wandering around again. That's when I got a lot worse,
started coughing up lots of blood and finally, thank god,
I got to die, and I'm telling you, it was great.
No pain, no job to go to, real quiet and cool
down in the grave. Then, after only four days,
it seemed a helluva lot shorter, the next thing I know
I'm being yanked out of there by good ol' Jesus,
and I'm all wrapped up like the mummy,
and everybody's yelling and screaming and happy
except me. Of course, now, Jesus is long gone,
but I still feel like crap and I saw some blood
on my pillowcase this morning, so I guess now
I have to die all over again and that's really going
to suck. I was afraid that when I die again real soon,
my sisters would run and get Jesus to ruin all my peace
and quiet again, but I heard just the other day
the Romans finally caught up with him
and plan to nail him to the cross quick as they can,
and, frankly, I don't blame them one little bit.
Why can't these religious nuts just leave
the rest of us well enough alone?

Divorce, Car Accidents, and Cancer

It's getting pretty dark.
Your pot-bellied uncle
puts down his beer bottle
and winds up to throw
a whiffle ball past you.
It's 1966 and you're in
his backyard outside
Baltimore; the Orioles
game is on the porch
radio. Your mom and
your aunt are on lawn
chairs under the trees
smoking Pall Malls,
drinking whiskey sours,
and yelling at your sister
and your three cousins
that it's time to get
out of the pool.

They've been gone for years,
all these people, what with
divorce, car accidents,
and cancer. You can't
remember now if you hit
your uncle's fastball, just as
you couldn't see the future
back then. Hell, you were only
ten years old, young enough
to think you could handle
anything thrown at you.

Fairlane 500

What Kerouac Wrote

Your bladder ain't what it used to be,
can't make the drive all the way home
anymore from anywhere, it seems.
You're at a convenience store now,
waiting desperately to take the worst leak
of your life. You've just spent four hours drinking
Pabst Blue Ribbon with some former students
and being the oldest guy by twenty years
at a weirdo music bar where everyone had
black framed glasses and clothes
you would have been ashamed of back
in the 70's. As you shift your weight
back and forth and eye the gray men's room door,
you think it's true what Kerouac wrote,
that Saturday night is dense and tragic
all over America and if the asshole inside
doesn't hurry up, there's going to be a tragedy
right there in your pants. You tell yourself now
at fifty, as you give yourself a furtive little squeeze
that you hope the security camera doesn't see,
that you're way too old for this kind of shit;
wonder how many more Saturday nights
you can spend peeing behind dumpsters
and Sunday mornings groping for the Excedrin.
Then you hear the toilet flush, some shuffling,
and the faucet turn on behind the door. You relax
a little bit, assure yourself that you can hold out
a little longer, start checking the cooler to see if
this crappy place sells anything but Budweiser
or that god awful Miller Lite.

God Blessed Us

If I Have Everything I Need

She's probably less than half my age,
cute as hell, calls me "hon" and brings
more iced tea without me asking. I like
the way she has her hair pushed back behind
her ear, and leans in close to take my order,
the soft fragrance of her soap, the silver
necklace on her skin. She asks if I want
the salmon again tonight and I say yes,
that I read somewhere that it was good
for me, try to give her my best smile.
I watch her walk away, her waist, her hips,
her ass, can't imagine she doesn't know
it's not the food that brings me here every night.

Back with my meal, she asks me if I have
everything I need. I tell her that it looks great
again tonight, am about to ask her if she ever thinks
about that salmon swimming upstream for miles
dodging grizzly bears the whole way just to spawn,
when she stops for a moment and says, Yeah,
my grandfather always orders the same thing, too.
I guess you old guys are all alike, then walks away again.
This time I can't look up, just stare at the lump of fish
on my plate, squeeze the slice of lemon until my fingers hurt
and it's way past dry.

SEAFARERS HALL

Crooner Al Martino Dies At 82

My grandmother took me to see him
sing, I remember, in a crowded ballroom
on the Steel Pier in Atlantic City back
in the summer of 1966. She was tiny,
a quiet woman who, all my relatives said,
never loved her second husband for a minute,
but she was a young widow with two little kids
and he had lots of overtime at Bethlehem Steel
with the war on, so they got married one afternoon
downtown, moved into their own fine row house
near the streetcar line in east Baltimore.

After the show, we went to see the famous
diving horse out on the Pier. Even as a kid,
I could tell the poor thing didn't dive at all,
but that he was shoved off that ledge, and
as I stood there holding my grandmother's hand,
I knew he managed to hit that pool of water so hard,
so smack dead center, only because he wasn't really
given any other choice at all.

YOU CAN NEVER GET TOO LOW -
WHEN YOU'RE SO DAMN HIGH
— ON THE BLESSED HELLRIDE

Outliving Elvis

Detroit, he whispered, goddamn Detroit
when the repeated thuds, pings, pops
of the midnight gunfire on New Year's Eve
woke him and reminded him
to stay away from the windows.

His girlfriend moved even closer,
tucked the top of her thigh
into the back of his knee.
He really knew how great she was,
the best of his best Texas days.
She even moved to Detroit to be with him,
where her darkest eyes and hair made her
pretty enough to be a car show hostess.
She was still, and they listened
in silence to the ongoing shooting.

He'd heard there was a snowstorm
predicted to blow in from the West
the day after tomorrow,
and after this listless two-week break
he'd be back teaching prep school kids
who mostly didn't give a shit,
grading essays that pained him
even more than the Visa card bill
at 17.9% interest that wouldn't go away.

She moved across his right shoulder
and kissed him just below the ear,
said, This is the year you outlive Elvis.
He grinned in the darkness
despite the sporadic gunshots.

He turned to hold her face to face,
relaxing with a lull in the firing
oblivious to when it might start again.

At 59

I find myself driving around
western Kansas, pausing to pee
and eat gas station burritos
in little towns with big names
like Ulysses and Syracuse.

I pull off the highway to take
a photo of a small roadside cross
that marks a car wreck death.
My lens zooms in and out
on a world so flat and spacious
that it almost makes me believe
it can go on forever.

MIDDLETOWN
OHIO
USA

A Beard Like John Berryman's

He's got a beard like John Berryman's,
a bottle of Bud Light and a pack of Camels
on the bar in front of him and he's blowing
the most perfect smoke rings I've ever seen.
When the barmaid comes with my beer,
he tells her that he has a question.
On the Dick Van Dyke Show, he says,
Mary Tyler Moore had really big boobs,
but then on her own show she didn't.
What do you think happened to them?
The barmaid looks at him, hands on hips,
tells him she doesn't have a fucking clue,
never thinks about Mary Tyler Moore's boobs,
then asks him to stop blowing smoke rings
all the time, it's driving her up the goddamn wall.
When she walks away, he starts blowing them again
right away, and I take my first swallow of beer, linger
a few moments watching the rings disappear into the bottles
all displayed so brightly there behind the bar.

Wasted

She slept on her couch, was still there
in the morning, wrapped in a blanket
and hugging her little dog. She mumbled
something about coffee, gestured
toward the kitchen. I was stirring
in some sugar when she turned down
the tv, and yelled out that she'd called
a limo service to take me to the airport,
they'd be here in about an hour or so,
I'd better shower and pack. Then she turned
the tv up even louder than before.

The day before we'd been drinking heavy
at her brother's birthday party, ended
up after dark real wasted out in the woods
with a bunch of people I didn't know.
She grabbed a blanket and a bottle
of wine, took me off by the hand
behind some trees where she started
kissing me. I wanted to kiss her back,
but I felt too drunk or something,
just laid there real still trying to hold
her tight enough to maybe stop time itself,
but it was no good. She pulled herself on top
of me, pushed down hard on my shoulders.
When the hell are you going to ask me to marry you?
she asked in the same voice she used with her dog
when he peed on the carpet. Can you please
just tell me when you're going to get around to it?
I wanted so badly to tell her, but by then she was sitting
on my chest and I could barely breathe.

In The Balls

It was a helluva good party, that's for sure.
Beowulf and his guys got back from Denmark
that afternoon. Elated, we yelled and hugged,
some even cried. We unloaded the ship-
all the horses, war gear, and treasure-
then brought out the best mead, started
drinking heavy while Beowulf told us
about that asshole Grendel and his bitch
mother, how he kicked their asses real good.
We cheered and whistled, then drank a toast
to good old King Hrothgar, that his troubles,
that all our troubles, were at an end,
and we kept on boozing and carousing
all night, as if we believed it were true.

Now the sun was trying to come up,
with just a few Vikings passed out
here and there in the hall. I saw Beowulf
himself standing alone on the hearth
staring down at the fire that was almost out.
I walked over, asked the big guy how he was doing.
He was quiet for a moment, then shook
his head slowly and said, Grendel kicked me
in the balls just as I was I ripping his fucking arm off.
It hurt like hell but everyone was so happy
that I didn't want to say anything. That night
Hrothgar set me up with two hot Danish chicks,
but I couldn't do a thing, then or ever since,
if you know what I mean. He put his head down
on the fireplace ledge, and I nodded in horror,
tried to put my arm around his giant shoulders.
I looked down to see that he was kicking at the fire,
gently at first, but then harder and harder,
but nothing at all was happening.

GOD BLESS AMERICA!

They Got To Stay

His wife had served the papers by surprise
the other day, so he had to get out, even though
it was snowing like hell. He didn't have much
stuff, mostly some garbage bags full of sheets
and towels, a few boxes of books, and a couple
laundry baskets full of neatly folded clothes.
We carried that out to his car, careful not to slip
and fall, heads down against the wind. He told me
there was food on the kitchen table, that he wanted
to check upstairs one more time. All I could find
were some cookies next to a bunch of photos
of his two children. Damn cute kids, red hair and toothy
smiles with the orthodontist bills still years away.
He came in and I told him not to forget the pictures,
that he should put them in a bag or something
to protect them. They got to stay, he said
as he arranged the pictures into a stack. Some shit
about community property my wife's lawyer says.
He seemed to hesitate for just a second, then suddenly
He screamed God damn her and wound up and threw
the whole pile across the room. We watched them flutter
in silence to the floor. When the last one reached the ground,
he put on his ski cap and said calmly, Let's get out of here.
Let that bitch worry about picking them up. I stuffed
some Oreos in my pocket and followed him out into the cold.

Some Real Asshole Baptists

I knew it was him right away –
the white robe, the wispy beard,
the crown of thorns. Holy shit,
I said, as he stood in my doorway
and handed me my pizza, then felt myself
turning red. It's OK, he told me, no worries.
I get that all the time. I handed him a twenty,
noticed a faint odor of vinegar, asked him how
everything was going. Well, he said with a shrug,
except for some real asshole Baptists and
a few perverted priests, the Savior thing is going
pretty well, but the economy really sucks
right now, so I'm doing this during the week
to help make ends meet. He started to count back
my change, but I told him to keep it, keep it all,
only wished I had more to give him. He nodded
and said he knew what that was like, and I gave him
a gentle tap on the shoulder, said, You take it real easy, Jesus.
I watched his sandals thwack lightly across the puddles
to the Honda Civic parked at the curb. Before he got in,
he turned to me, made the sign of the cross, yelled, Bless you,
my son, I'll be back sometime for sure, then drove off.
I went back inside, got a fresh beer and some napkins,
felt so good I didn't even start swearing when I realized
I was out of crushed red pepper and that Jesus forgot
my goddamn cheesey bread.

Jesus
is
Lord
AHS '10

When The Heat Became Too Much

Even though we had a backyard pool,
my mother never learned to swim,
always stayed in the shallow end.
Finished with the ironing and laundry,
and having done the grocery shopping,
she had her friends over on summer afternoons.
They relaxed on the poolside lounges,
drank tall vodka tonics, munched salty peanuts.
In a few minutes they'd be laughing real loud;
you could hear them all the way inside the house.
When the heat became too much, they'd climb
into the pool, careful not to wet their hair.
Oh, that feels good they'd say when they got out,
rubbing on another coat of Coppertone,
sipping on a freshened drink.
When the trees caught the sun, they'd slip
on their sandals, dab on some lipstick,
start to walk toward their cars.
Time to get dinner on the table my mom would say,
gathering towels and glasses until it looked
as if no one had been there at all.

"Don't ask what your Country can do for you, But rather What can you do for your Country.

Don't Be Absurd

It's as if my dream were directed by Truffaut
or Godard – foggy Paris in black & white
with yellow English sub-titles and I'm standing
on a bridge with who must be Albert Camus,
wry grin, trench coat with collar turned up,
cigarette dangling. If I jumped off this bridge
into the Seine, he asks me, would you jump
in to save me? I stare at him through the mist
to see if this is real, if he's serious, but before
I can figure out how to say don't be absurd
in French, he flicks his cigarette away, pushes
past me and vaults over the ledge. I run after him,
stare over the edge, see him reaching back toward me,
but well out of reach, spinning, falling, then a splash.

That's, of course, when I wake up. Holy shit,
I say to myself, hesitate for a second to make sure
it's just a dream, but something's still not right.
I throw off the covers which seem way too heavy
and the mattress squishes as I sit up and swing
my feet to the floor. I turn on the lamp, rub my eyes,
realize I need to pee real badly. As I shuffle
toward the door, I try to figure out how I'm going
to get the damned cigarette smoke out of the room,
and where I'm going to throw my wet pajamas.

When I die, don't come, I wouldn't want a leaf
to turn away from the sun . . .

I knew the cemetery where we buried Frank O'Hara,
had been there years earlier with him to lay flowers
at Pollock's grave. Frank told me that day he couldn't imagine
living past forty, that he wanted to die young and still
beautiful like Keats or Shelley.

Just another summer weekend out of Manhattan,
we'd been at the disco for hours, glad to be away
from that blowhard Virgil Thomson, drinking and dancing.
Frank yelled to me over the voice of some queen wailing
"These Boots Were Made For Walking" that he never wanted
to sleep again, but I managed to talk him into leaving about two.
Then it's all drunken darkness, the broken-down beach taxi,
and Frank wandering off down toward the water. I remember
seeing him unsteady in the headlights of that second dune buggy,
somehow neither moving into its path nor trying to get out of the way.
Then the collision, the chaos, his last days in that dreary Long Island
hospital.
He was forty years old, still more sadly beautiful than Keats or Shelley.

Blizzards

Lee wanted me to meet his ex-girlfriend,
Jennifer, so we borrowed a car, an old Datsun
everybody called the Batmobile, and drove
over to Austin. When she came out
on the porch, she took one look at him
and said, What the fuck are you doing here?
He told her calmly that he wanted his friend Dave
to meet her. She told him that he and his little friend
Dave could go to hell for all she cared.

I could tell things weren't going too well,
so I walked down to the curb,
stood with my hands in my pockets
watching the traffic go by. Lee came back
in a few minutes, we got in the Batmobile
without saying anything and drove off.

We stopped at the Dairy Queen in Elgin
for Oreo Blizzards. Lee said the summer
after he graduated from high school
he'd get her a cherry Coke with lime
from the Sonic and pick her up
from her lifeguarding shift at the country club.
Then they'd go somewhere and screw
like crazy in the front seat of his sister's truck.
Sounds good, I told him, sounds real good.
She's a crazy bitch now, he said, but I still love her.
When we got back to College Station about dark,
the rest of my Blizzard had melted,
the ice cream no longer recognizable,
just a watery syrup with dark bits
of something sweet settled at the bottom.

The Mary

You've learned over the years that every night
in every hotel bar everywhere there's a woman
who looks just like Mary Travers, the Mary
of Peter, Paul and Mary. Not the young,
skinny, ironed-straight hair Mary singing
"If I Had A Hammer" in a black & white video,
but the older, sort of beat-up Mary doing
"I Dig Rock n' Roll Music" on one of those
shameless PBS fundraisers. She's always sitting
at the bar with a big glass of white wine
and her laptop open, talking loudly to some guy
with a loosened tie about market share or
sales quotas or how bad the Atlanta airport is.

When you pay your tab and start to leave
you're always tempted to tell her how much
you liked her music when you were a kid,
and then ask if "Puff The Magic Dragon" was
really about marijuana and if there was ever
any three–way sex with Peter and Paul,
but you're always tired and a little drunk
and you want to catch the rest of *The Daily Show*
back in your room, so you keep on walking
past her humming "Leaving On A Jet Plane"
and telling yourself you can always talk to her
tomorrow night in whatever hotel bar you want.

FOR SALE
MA E OFFER
1937-2144861

Even The Fallen

They must have killed Chet Baker
before they pushed him out
that Amsterdam hotel window
because angels, even the fallen
kind, always have wings.

HOOVER

Still Red

Our lease is coming up, his girlfriend said.
They were driving home after their regular
Tuesday night dinner out, stuffed with Rib-eyes
and loaded baked potatoes. How soon?
he asked. End of the month, she replied.
He started to brake for a red light. She asked him
what he thought. He looked to his left
at the old K-Mart building. He tried to think
how long it had been out of business
but couldn't remember. I'd like more space,
I guess, he told her, still staring at the big empty
parking lot. Me, too, she said. More space
might help us. He looked up at the traffic light.
Still red. He moved the gearshift to neutral
then back to first gear. Jesus, he said.
Does this light ever change? I know, she answered.
It feels like we've been sitting here forever.

Hitchhiker

I was driving the high desert, south
out of Klamath Falls into California
When I picked up a hitchhiker
just outside Alturas. I could see
he didn't have any arms, so I opened
the door for him, helped him in,
clicked his seatbelt, too.
The whole way down Route 395
to Susanville, he didn't say a damn thing,
just sat there all quiet, staring
straight ahead. When I let him off,
I waved good-bye as he crossed the road
and started walking back in the direction we came.
When he didn't wave back, I realized
maybe he hadn't been hitchhiking at all.

Still Up In The Attic

The trains didn't stop at my hometown anymore,
but on firefly nights with windows wide open,
I could hear them rolling all the way down along
the Hudson, south to Grand Central or north to Albany,
then west to places I had never been. It was my world
then, the tract house neighborhood full of kids, the A&P
and Western Auto, the Tastee-Freeze, and our elementary school.
We played softball all summer long, games of ghost runners
and poison fields, bought icy, little green bottles of Coke
at the Sunoco station on the bike ride home. Our dads were back
from the war and the G.I. Bill to computer jobs at IBM
and highballs before dinner, tomato gardens in the backyard.
Moms kept house on coffee and cigarettes, served meals
like clockwork with church every Sunday.

But the summer games became summer jobs scooping ice cream
or painting houses, then the kids all scattered for college, or jobs
in Houston, Charlotte, or Atlanta. I heard the A&P got torn down
and the school closed, came to realize my parents were forgetting
any news I gave them on the phone, ran out of good excuses
for not getting home more often. They had our house air-conditioned
a few years before they sold it and moved down to Tampa for good
and died soon after. I came home the last time to get my yearbooks
and baseball glove still up in the attic, and I'm sure that down by the
river
the trains were still running like always, but I couldn't hear them
anymore,
my bedroom windows now closed up tight.

All Kinds Of Shit

I got no wife and kids, and no God,
but a year ago I had cancer;
things sure didn't look too good.
I made it through chemo, lost
my hair, a few pounds, and my lunch
some days, then they took out
most of my right lung, left me
in the hospital for three weeks
hooked up to all kinds of shit
waiting for some leak to close.
I never smoked or anything,
don't know why I got so sick.
The doctors said sometimes
things like this just happen.

I'm doing OK now, back to work
and all that. I still like to drink beer
and watch movies on weekends,
try to get out to lots of ballgames
in the summer, barely notice
the missing lung. Yeah, life's
pretty much the same except
I don't dry myself in front of the mirror
these days, don't need those big scars
to make me think about all the things
I've lost and won't be getting back.

I
SATAN

After My Funeral

If you have people back to your house
for food and drinks after my funeral,
please don't invite any assholes, especially
bosses or landlords. Be sure to serve
longneck bottles of Pabst Blue Ribbon
and feed everybody pizza, with plenty
of anchovies on every slice. Please don't let
anybody in who shows up with one of those
shitty veggie trays with ranch dressing from Kroger,
and play Bill Evans in the background,
but not so loud that everybody has to scream.
Make people talk about Hollywood movies
or Hemingway novels or Pollock paintings -
any of the good things in life. Kick out anyone
who dares mention their crappy job, or Christian Science
or the fucking Chicago Cubs, and when people start to leave,
say good-bye to everyone for me like you'll never ever see them again.

At the end...
there is
Judgement

Acknowledgments:

These works have appeared in:
Nerve Cowboy, The Chiron Review, Slipstream, Children, Churches & Daddies, Midwestern Gothic, Fight These Bastards, Naked Knuckle, FreeFall, The Quirk, Fox Cry Review, Misfit Magazine, and Blotterature.

David J. Thompson grew up in Hyde Park, New York, and currently lives in Chapel Hill, North Carolina. He is a former prep school teacher and coach who worked at schools in New York, Texas, Florida, and Michigan. His interests include movies, jazz, and minor league baseball. Please visit his photo website at ninemilephoto.com.